Enid Blyton's
Enchanted Tales

THE WIZARD
WHO WASN'T

Enid Blyton's
Enchanted Tales

The Magical Shop
Return to the Magical Shop
The Faraway Tree Adventure
The Wizard who Wasn't
Adventures in Fairyland
Magic in Fairyland

Enid Blyton's Enchanted Tales

THE WIZARD
WHO WASN'T

Illustrated by Robin Lawrie

RED FOX

A Red Fox Book

Published by Random House Children's Books
20 Vauxhall Bridge Road, London SW1V 2SA

A division of The Random House Group Ltd
London Melbourne Sydney Auckland
Johannesburg and agencies throughout the world

1 3 5 7 9 10 8 6 4 2

Red Fox edition 1994
This edition published by Red Fox 2000

Printed and bound in Great Britain by
Cox and Wyman Ltd, Reading, Berkshire

THE RANDOM HOUSE GROUP Limited Reg. No. 954009

www.randomhouse.co.uk

ISBN 0 09 940805 8

Contents

CHAPTER ONE

Bobadil becomes a Wizard

Bobadil was a pixie, and a very smart one, too. He knew how many beans made five, and how much a pennyworth of sweets cost, and all the rest of the things taught at a good pixie school.

But he couldn't seem to find any work to do, now that he had left school, and was all on his own. Nobody wanted him, and Bobadil was getting very much upset about it.

'I shall have to leave this town, and try somewhere else,' thought Bobadil at last. So he packed up his things, put them in a big red handkerchief, slung them over his back, and set out.

He hadn't gone very far, before he saw a great crowd of pixies and gnomes standing at the street corner, talking very excitedly.

'What's the matter?' asked Bobadil.

'Oh, haven't you heard?' said one.

'Why, the great enchanter, Thinkalot, is passing through here this afternoon, and we all want to see him.'

Well, Bobadil thought he really must stop and see Thinkalot, so he popped his bundle down, and climbed up a lamp-post. No sooner had he done that than he heard the sound of trumpets, and round the corner came a magnificent carriage, drawn by six white donkeys. In the carriage sat the enchanter Thinkalot, frowning hard at a book he was reading, and taking no notice at all of any of the cheering people.

'My, isn't he grand!' cried everyone, tremendously impressed. 'Just look at him, reading his magic books, and sitting there so grand and powerful!'

Bobadil thought the enchanter was wonderful, and he wished with all his heart that he could be an enchanter too, instead of an out-of-work pixie. He slid down the lamppost, and ran after the carriage, determined to follow it until it was out of sight.

On went the six white donkeys, trotting the carriage along at a smart pace, and on went Bobadil, fixing his eyes on the enchanter's tall, black hat, and star-patterned robe. He thought he looked tremendously grand, and the little pixie longed to have a hat and robe just exactly the same.

'If I were dressed like that,' he thought, 'I should be able to get plenty of work, for people wouldn't dare to refuse me!'

He ran along after the carriage, which gradually drew ahead of him, and was soon away in the distance. Bobadil still

ran on, keeping his eyes on the cloud of
dust that was now all he could see of the
enchanter's carriage.

He wasn't looking at all where he was
going, so it wasn't surprising that he
suddenly tripped over something and fell
bump, onto his little turned-up nose. He
picked himself up, dusted his coat, and
looked to see what it was that he had
fallen over. It was a book! A great big red
and black book, and on the front was
written –

'Thinkalot's Magic Book.'

'Oh my!' said Bobadil. 'The enchanter's

own book of magic! It must have fallen out of the carriage. I say! What a find!'

He opened the book curiously, and looked inside. To his great astonishment, the same thing was written on every single page!

'Take this book back to its owner. Take this book back to its owner.' That was what Bobadil read ever so many times.

'How can I take it back?' wondered Bobadil. 'The enchanter is miles away by now. I shouldn't have thought it was of much use anyhow, with just that one sentence written in it!'

He put the book under his arm, and went on his way again. He hadn't gone very far before he saw a cloud of dust in the distance, that became bigger as he watched.

'Something's coming this way,' said Bobadil to himself. He watched to see what it was, and was very much surprised to see that it was the enchanter's carriage coming slowly back again, with the enchanter leaning out of it, looking closely at every piece of road he passed.

'Oho!' said Bobadil. 'He's missed his magic book. What a grand man he looks to be sure!'

The enchanter stopped when he saw Bobadil and spoke to him.

'Have you seen a big magic book?' he asked.

'Here it is,' said Bobadil, taking it from under his arm. 'It's a funny sort of book, I must say! It's got no magic in it at all.'

The enchanter smiled. 'Oh yes, it has,' he said. 'But you couldn't see it. Look now, whilst I hold it in my own hand.'

Bobadil looked at the page that the enchanter showed him, and to his surprise saw that now it was full of curious drawings, and wonderful magic words that he had never heard of.

'My!' he cried. 'That's a funny thing.'

'What would you like as a reward for finding my book?' asked the enchanter.

'Oh!' said Bobadil, most excited. '*I* know what I'd like, Sir Enchanter.'

'Speak on,' said Thinkalot.

'I'd like to have a tall black hat, and star-patterned robe like yours,' said Bobadil. 'You do look so very grand!'

'Very well,' said Thinkalot. 'You may have them.'

He said no more, but turned his donkeys round again, and drove quickly off, leaving Bobadil staring after him in surprise.

'Hie, hie,' cried the pixie, seeing the enchanter rapidly driving away. 'You haven't given me those clothes.'

The enchanter made no reply, and Bobadil felt dreadfully disappointed. He began to run after the carriage when he suddenly tripped, and down he went again, head over heels.

'Now, what tripped me up *that* time?' wondered Bobadil crossly. He sat up and looked – and he saw that he had tumbled over a long robe that wrapped him about from his head to his heels – a star-patterned robe, just like the enchanter's.

'*There's* magic for you!' said Bobadil in astonishment. 'Have I got a big black hat, too?'

He felt to see, and yes, he had, set on the top of his little round head.

'Ha,' said the pixie, getting onto his feet again. 'I'm very grand now, I am. I'll make everyone think I am a great wizard, and if I can't get a job to do now, well, I'll eat my fine new hat.'

He decided to go straight on, and take the road to Twisty-Town, a little place a good way off, that would not have heard either of Bobadil the pixie or Thinkalot the Enchanter.

He put his best foot foremost, and marched along singing, feeling as grand as a jay-bird in his fine new clothes. All day he went along, through woods and fields, over hills, and down dales, till at last, when evening came, he saw Twisty-Town, set up on a hill, dyed red in the evening sun.

CHAPTER TWO

The Twisty–Town Adventure

'It would be a good idea if I could find something to ride on,' said Bobadil. 'It doesn't look quite the thing to go into a town on foot if I am a wizard.'

He looked about, but he could see nothing at all that would do.

'Heigho!' he sighed. 'I must go without, I suppose.'

'Go without what, Master Wizard?' asked a shy little voice.

Bobadil turned, and saw a brown rabbit peeping out of his hole, his two big ears standing upright. 'Go without something to carry me into Twisty-

Town,' said Bobadil.

'Would I do?' asked the rabbit. 'I'm big for my age, and I'd like to come with you. I could carry you beautifully.'

Bobadil was delighted. A rabbit is very soft to ride on, and gets along at a fine pace. 'Better than six donkeys!' thought the pixie. 'And won't take much feeding either.'

'I'll let you come with me,' he said. 'Come here, and I'll jump on your back. Take me into Twisty-Town, and remember this – if anyone asks you anything about me, you tell them I'm Bobadil the Wizard, very clever and powerful. See?'

The rabbit promised, and the two set off, Bobadil finding it very comfortable indeed on the rabbit's back. He soon came to the streets of Twisty-Town, and looked at the curious winding ways all around him. Not a straight road was there in the town, and when Bobadil went round a corner, the only thing he saw was *another* corner. The houses too were curiously shaped, with twisty roofs and crooked chimneys.

When the people saw Bobadil in his tall wizard hat, and strange cloak, they

came running out of their houses to follow him.

'A wizard, a wizard!' they cried.

Bobadil enjoyed it all very much, and went slowly through the town, his head up in the air, as grand as anything. Suddenly he heard someone calling to him in a very loud voice.

'Are you a real wizard?' said the voice.

'Try me and see,' said Bobadil, feeling a little bit afraid.

'If you are a real wizard,' said the little man with the loud voice, 'perhaps you can help to solve a mystery for us.'

'I don't mind trying,' said Bobadil, obligingly. 'What's the mystery?'

'Come into our town hall, and I'll tell you,' said the little man.

He led the way, and after they had turned fifteen different corners, Bobadil saw the funny little town hall. He followed the man in, and tied up the rabbit by the door.

In the hall were ten Twisty-Town people, all looking very worried.

'I've brought a wizard,' said the little

man. 'Maybe he'll help us.'

'Let me tell you our trouble,' said the chief. 'We've had a terrible robbery. You see, it was like this. The old witch Hobble-round, in return for a good deed we did to her, sent our town a bag of gold, which would never be empty, however much we took from it.'

'And we put it away in this cupboard,' said another, 'and locked it up. We just used it when we wanted it – and now it's gone, and we don't know who's stolen it!'

'So could you use your magic and tell us who has got it?' asked a third.

'Certainly, certainly,' said Bobadil, wondering whatever he was going to do. 'Have you any idea who the robber may be?'

'Well,' said the chief, slowly, 'the man who brought you here says he saw his neighbour, the brownie Merry-eyes, stealing into this hall late last night. We asked Merry-eyes, whether he *was* here, but he says no, he was in bed.'

'I tell you it *was* Merry-eyes,' said the little man, spitefully. 'I saw him myself. That wizard, if he is one, will soon tell you the same.'

The little man looked at him so queerly that Bobadil began to feel he knew he was just a pixie, and not a wizard after all. He said nothing, and let the chief take him to a little tumble-down cottage to sleep for the night.

'I've told everybody what you told me to say,' said the rabbit, excitedly, when he and Bobadil were alone. 'Are you going to do anything magic here, Master?'

'I hope so,' said Bobadil, with a sigh. 'I must just think hard now, bunny, so don't disturb me.'

Bobadil had hardly begun to think, when there came a knock at the door, and in came the little man with the loud voice.

'I've just come to tell you that I *know* Merry-eyes took that bag of gold,' said the visitor, grinning. 'And you'd better tell everyone so too, because you'll be quite safe then. *I* don't believe you're a wizard, though you've got a tall hat and a fine cloak. I never saw a wizard with a turned-up nose before, no I didn't. Why don't you use your magic to turn it down the proper way?'

'What do you mean by talking to me like this?' asked Bobadil, trying to sound very stern.

'Yah!' said the unpleasant little man. 'You do as I tell you, or I'll tell everyone you're not a wizard. See?'

'And suppose I *am* a wizard?' said Bobadil.

'Ho! Ho!' laughed the other. 'If you *are*,

you'll find out for certain who stole the gold, then I'll know you're cleverer than I think you are!'

He slammed the door, and went off chuckling. Bobadil didn't like him at all. He began to think very hard again, and soon he smiled. He had thought of a very good plan.

'I'll go to sleep now,' he yawned. 'And in the morning I'll see if I think my idea will really catch the thief.'

He lay down on his bed, cuddled up to the rabbit, and fell fast asleep.

CHAPTER THREE

The Bunny's Tail

Next day Bobadil told the rabbit his plan.

'You must help me,' he said. 'Do just what I tell you, and we shall soon find out the thief. Go and buy a bag of white flour, and then come back to me.'

The rabbit scampered out, and soon came back with the flour.

'Turn round,' said Bobadil, 'I'm going to rub your little white tail in the flour.'

The rabbit was very much astonished, but he did as he was told. Bobadil rubbed his tail in the flour, until it was as full as could be of the fine white stuff.

'Now listen,' said Bobadil. 'I am going to give out a notice that everyone in Twisty-Town must go to the town hall this afternoon, and pull your tail gently. I won't let them hurt you.'

'But how will that discover the thief?' asked the rabbit, puzzled.

'I shall say that when the thief pulls your tail, you will at once cry out, "The thief! The thief!"' said Bobadil.

'Oh, but *I* shan't know when the thief pulls my tail!' said the rabbit in alarm.

'Don't get worried,' said Bobadil. 'You keep quiet and say nothing all the time. Leave everything to me.'

He sent out his message, and everyone was most impressed.

'What a wonderful wizard he must be to find out who the thief is by making us all pull his rabbit's tail,' said the people.

That afternoon all the folk of Twisty-Town turned up at the town hall. Bobadil made them stand in a long line outside, and go in one at a time, alone, whilst he stood outside the door.

'When you have pulled my rabbit's

tail,' he said, 'go into the big room on the other side of the hall, put your hands behind you, and wait for me.'

One by one the people all went in, and gently pulled the little white bobtail of the patient rabbit. He sat as quiet as could be, and never made a sound. When they had pulled his tail, the people went into the other room, put their hands behind their backs, and waited for Bobadil.

'I haven't heard the rabbit cry out yet, have you?' whispered the people to one another. 'There must be hardly anyone left now to pull the rabbit's tail.'

At last everyone had passed through the hall, and were standing with their hands behind their backs in the big room nearby. Bobadil came to them.

'Yah! Yah!' cried the little man with the loud voice, mockingly. 'The rabbit didn't cry out! You're a fine wizard, aren't you!'

Bobadil said nothing, but he went behind the people and had a good look at everyone's hands. They were all white with flour except one person's – and that was the little man with the loud voice.

Bobadil grinned to himself, and went to face the folk again. He drew a circle on the ground, said all the magic words he knew, which wasn't very many, whilst the people watched breathlessly.

'Yah!' said the unpleasant little man again. 'You can't take us in like that! *You* don't know who the thief is! The rabbit didn't make a sound!'

'And I'll tell you why he didn't!' said Bobadil in a deep voice. 'It was because the thief was too afraid to pull the rabbit's tail!'

'Didn't he pull it, didn't he pull it?' cried the people.

'Bah!' said the little man. 'How do *you* know? You weren't in the room to see! I tell you it was Merry-eyes who stole the gold, and I say you're a pretty poor wizard if you don't know that.'

'Listen, people,' said Bobadil. 'My rabbit's tail was covered with white flour. As you pulled it your hands became covered with white. Now Merry-eyes, step forward and show me your hand.'

Merry-eyes stepped forward, and showed his right hand, with which he had pulled the rabbit's tail. It was white and floury!

'You are not the thief,' said Bobadil. 'Next one, please.'

One by one the people came and showed their hands to Bobadil, and each time he found them white and said, '*You* are not the thief.'

The horrid little man got behind all the others, and began to shiver and shake. He hoped that Bobadil might perhaps not see him. But Bobadil wasn't quite so silly. He left him right till last and then grabbed hold of him.

'Show your hands,' he said.

The little man was forced to hold them out. They were both as brown as berries!

Not a speck of white was on them!

'You have not pulled my rabbit's tail,'
said Bobadil, sternly. 'Why not? Were you
afraid to? Were you afraid that he would
cry out "The thief! The thief!"?'

The little man shivered and shook, and
said never a word.

'Where is that bag of gold?' asked Bobadil suddenly in his very loudest voice. 'Tell me before I turn you into a black beetle.'

This made the little man shiver and shake all the more, and he suddenly burst out crying, and said: 'Oh, great wizard, be merciful to me! I will tell you where I have hidden the magic bag of gold and you shall take it.'

When the people heard this, they were most astonished, and very angry. Bobadil waved them away, and followed the little man out of the hall, and into the twisty street. Everybody ran behind, all talking excitedly.

At last the little man came to an old hollow tree, put his hand right down into it, and drew up – the magic bag of gold! How everyone gasped to see it!

The chief of the town took the bag, put his hand in, and brought out a fistful of gleaming yellow gold. He turned to Bobadil.

'We thank you very much, Sir Wizard,' he said. 'Will you accept this as a return

for your help?'

Well, Bobadil had never seen such a lot of gold in all his life, and he didn't mind accepting it at all.

'I will take it with pleasure,' he said, and put it into his pocket. Then the chief took the shivering little thief, and marched him off to the town hall again, to decide what punishment he should have, and all the people followed.

Bobadil jumped onto his rabbit, and went off in the opposite direction, humming a tune, as happy as a sandboy.

'We'll make our fortunes at this rate,' he said to the bunny. 'It's as easy as anything!'

CHAPTER FOUR

The Gobble–up Witch

Bobadil travelled on for some time until he came to another town. To his surprise, as he rode through it nobody came to follow him. The houses were tightly shut, the windows were closed, and not a child or dog was in the streets.

'This is strange,' said Bobadil. 'Where is everyone on this fine day? Surely not shut up in their houses.'

He went to one house and knocked. There was no answer. He knocked again. Still no one came. He called. That made no difference either.

Bobadil went to all the houses in the street and rang the bells and knocked – but nobody opened the doors or even looked out of the window.

'Hey!' called Bobadil. 'Where is everybody? Is there no one here who can give a visitor a drink of water?'

For a minute there was no answer.

Then a voice, frightened and shaking, came from one of the houses.

'Who are you?'

'I am Bobadil, the great wizard, who has just come from discovering the thief in Twisty-Town,' answered Bobadil in surprise.

A door opened cautiously and the head of an old gnome peeped out.

'You are not the witch Gobble-up in some new form?' he asked.

'Good gracious, no!' said Bobadil.

'Can't you see I am a wizard? Look at my hat and robe. What's the matter with everyone here?'

As he spoke, doors began to open up and down the street, and people began to creep out and come near to where Bobadil stood.

'I will tell you why we are so frightened,' said the old gnome. 'Our town is in the power of a horrible witch, and she has taken to eating some of us, or catching us as her servants. She is so clever that we never know when or how she is coming. She may come in the form of a horse, or a man, a rabbit, or even a stream of water. Whatever she touches on her way through the town becomes hers. So you see, when we see any stranger coming we go into our houses, shut our doors, and wait for the witch to pass.'

'Well, I am no witch,' said Bobadil. 'I am a wizard.'

'Do you know of any spell to get rid of a wicked witch?' asked the old gnome hopefully.

'I might,' said Bobadil. 'Where does she live?'

Just as he asked that there came a shout of terror and the people began to run for their lives.

'See!' cried the gnome, 'She is coming now and in her own shape. Run, Sir Wizard.'

Bobadil didn't run, although he felt very like it. He stayed where he was, and watched the witch come down the street on her broomstick. She was a hideous old woman, with bright green eyes and a very hooked nose.

'Good day to you, witch,' said Bobadil.

'Good day to yourself,' said the witch, stopping. 'I see you are a wizard?'

'And a very powerful one, too,' put in the rabbit, bravely.

'Ho, is that so?' said the witch. 'Can you change yourself into a roaring dragon?'

'Can *you*?' said Bobadil.

'Of course I can,' said the witch.

'Go on, then,' said Bobadil.

At once the witch turned into a fierce dragon, whose hot breath blew onto Bobadil and singed his hair.

'Wonderful, wonderful!' he cried. 'But pray turn into a witch again. You have set fire to my cloak with your burning breath.'

The dragon became a witch again, and laughed to see the hem of Bobadil's cloak smouldering. She reached her hand up in the air, and brought it down with a can of water in it, much to Bobadil's astonishment. He took it, and splashed a little onto his cloak to put the smouldering out.

'Ha!' said the witch. 'Can you change yourself into a giant?'

'Can *you*?' asked Bobadil, nervously.

'Watch and see,' answered the witch, and straightaway turned herself into a giant as high as the clouds, so that Bobadil had to lie down to see the great pink face, away up in the sky above him.

'Marvellous! Marvellous!' cried Bobadil. 'Change back into a witch again!'

The giant became old witch Gobble-up, and she grinned at him.

'Now let me see *you* do something!' she said.

'In a minute,' said Bobadil. 'I will do something that you cannot do.'

'What is that?' asked the witch in surprise.

'I will change myself into an egg!' said Bobadil.

'Pooh, that's easy!' said the witch, scornfully. 'Look at me!'

Bobadil looked, and before his eyes she changed into a hen's brown egg, lying on the floor at his feet. In a flash Bobadil stooped down to pick it up and smash it, hoping that would put an end to the witch once and for all. But she was too quick for him. In a second she changed back to her own form again and stood glaring at Bobadil.

'What do you want to pick that egg up for?' she asked, angrily.

'To examine such a marvel closely, of course,' answered Bobadil. 'I know *one* thing you couldn't change yourself into, old witch, and that is a blade of grass! Such a small thing is more difficult to turn into than a big thing, and I'm sure that is beyond your powers.'

41

The witch snorted, said a quick magic word and changed into a green blade of grass. Like a flash the rabbit pounced, and Bobadil saw him chewing hard.

'Ah, that's finished her,' he thought, but alas! Just as he was going to pat the rabbit on the back the witch re-appeared.

'Punish your rabbit, punish your rabbit!' she cried. 'He tried to eat me, and if he hadn't picked the wrong blade of grass, I should be dead by now. Quick, punish your rabbit.'

Bobadil hardly had time to think what to do, but he just managed to.

'Wicked rabbit!' he said, turning to the frightened bunny. 'We will roast you over a fire, and cook you for our dinner now. Witch, turn yourself into a fire, and you shall yourself roast this wicked rabbit!'

The cruel witch laughed to hear this and at once changed into a roaring fire. Quick as thought Bobadil snatched up the jug of water he had used to put out the smouldering of his robe, and poured it all over the fire. It fizzled – died down

– and went out. Nothing was left of it but a few black embers. Bobadil and the rabbit waited tremblingly to see if the witch would come back to life again – but she didn't!

'She's dead, she's dead!' cried the rabbit, and flung his front paws round Bobadil's neck.

When the people heard this they all came flocking out of their houses again and made a cheering ring round the clever pair. They took them to the market and gave them the finest dinner there that they had ever had.

'Never have we seen such a clever wizard before,' they cried. 'Give him a bag of gold and bid him good luck on his way. He has saved us from the wicked witch.'

Well, Bobadil was very pleased to take the bag of gold they gave him and add it to the other gold he had had from the folk of Twisty-Town. He said goodbye to the people and once again he and the rabbit started on their travels to make their fortunes.

CHAPTER FIVE

The Princess and the Red Goblin

For some days Bobadil went on travelling with his faithful little bunny and met with no adventures at all. Then, as he was passing through a wood, he thought he heard a sobbing and a crying. He stopped and listened. Yes, it was quite true.

He went in the direction of the sound and came to a tall tower, in the top of which was a fairy princess, leaning out of a window, sobbing bitterly. Her tears fell onto the ground below like rain.

'What is the matter?' asked Bobadil.

'Oh go away,' said the princess. 'You will get caught by the Red Goblin if you don't.'

'I will risk that,' said Bobadil. 'Tell me why you are crying.'

'I am crying because I am the goblin's

prisoner,' said the princess, 'and he wants to marry me. I love a noble prince, who comes every day to try and rescue me, but in vain. See, here he comes.'

Bobadil heard footsteps and saw a handsome prince nearby. The princess called out to him and begged him to tell Bobadil to run whilst there was time.

'Yes, go quickly,' said the prince sadly. 'I am in the goblin's power, too. He told me that if I could ask him to do anything he was not able to do he would set my princess free. He gave me twelve days to do this, and alas! Everything that I have so far asked him he has done. Today is my last chance, and I can think of nothing.'

'What have you asked him to do?' asked Bobadil.

'Well, I have asked him to build me a castle in a single night,' said the prince. 'I have asked him to bring me the most valuable necklace in the world. I have even asked him to give me a thousand soldiers of my own.'

'Did he do all this?' asked Bobadil, in astonishment.

'Oh yes,' said the prince with a sigh. 'The castle is quite near here, and the thousand soldiers are guarding it for me. I gave the necklace to my sweet little princess, but of what use are castles and soldiers to me, or necklaces to her, if I am not to marry her? We shall both be miserable all our lives long.'

'What else did you ask for?' said Bobadil.

'I asked for a hundred bags of gold,'

said the prince, 'and the most beautiful
and fastest horse in the world. I begged
him to get me a cloak that would make
me invisible when I put it on, and a
sword that would cut through anything.
I made him get me wings that I could
fasten to my ankles and fly as fast as a
swallow. All of these he got me and other
things besides.'

'Oho,' said Bobadil. 'If you will trust
yourselves to me, I think I can rescue you
both from the Red Goblin without much
difficulty.'

'Oh, wonderful wizard!' cried the
prince gratefully. 'If you can only do that
I will give you the hundred bags of gold.'

'A hundred bags of gold!' thought
Bobadil. 'Why, that would certainly
make my fortune.'

'The Red Goblin lives in a great cave in
the heart of the wood,' said the prince. 'I
have got to go to him in ten minutes to
ask him the twelfth thing. If he can do it,
he will straightaway come and marry the
princess, and I shall be killed. How are
you going to rescue us, wizard?'

'Change clothes with me, quickly,' said Bobadil. 'I am going in your place, and if I don't manage to ask the Goblin something he won't like I'll never try anything again.'

The Prince quickly changed clothes with Bobadil. He put on the cloak and tall hat, while Bobadil put on the prince's feathered hat and smart tunic. When he was ready, he turned to the prince.

'Follow me closely,' he said, 'and see what happens.'

The Prince did as he was told, and together the two made their way into the wood. They came at last to a deep cave guarded at the entrance by two fierce cats. Bobadil's bunny was frightened when he saw them and crouched down behind some bushes, whilst his master entered the cave, leaving the prince outside.

Bobadil walked boldly into the cave, looking for the Goblin. He came at last to a great hall, lit by a single star-shaped lamp in the middle. At the end of the hall sat the Red Goblin, a most unpleasant-looking creature.

'So you've come to make your last request,' said the Goblin. 'Well, can you ask me anything that I shall not do?'

'Yes,' answered Bobadil. 'I will ask you to do something that you will not do.'

'What is that?' grinned the Goblin, unbelievingly.

'This is my twelfth request,' said Bobadil. 'Can you go right away from here and never come back again?'

The Goblin sat upright at once when he heard what Bobadil said. For some time he said never a word. Then he frowned and began to bite his stumpy nails.

'Ho, ho,' said Bobadil. 'That is something you cannot do, Red Goblin . . . and remember what you said would happen if you didn't do what was asked. You promised you would leave the Princess to me, and let me take her away.'

The Red Goblin thought that the *Prince* was speaking to him. He had no idea that it was Bobadil.

'I will go away on one condition,' he said, grinning wickedly. 'If you promise not to marry the Princess yourself I will never bother you again.'

Bobadil smiled to himself when he heard this. *He* didn't want to marry the Princess, so he could safely promise.

'Very well, I promise,' he said, sighing

deeply to make the Goblin think that he was grieved about it. 'All I want is that the dear Princess shall be freed from the tower.'

'Free her, then!' suddenly shouted the Goblin, angrily. 'I am going right away now, but you will find it very difficult to get your precious Princess free, I promise you! And if you do you can't marry her, for you have vowed not to!'

With that he gave a yell, jumped straight up into the air, and vanished. Bobadil couldn't see where he went, and stood staring in amazement. Then he hurried out to tell the Prince what had happened.

But he found his way barred by the two fierce cats! They had let him in without so much as stirring a whisker, but they didn't mean to let him out again. They snarled at him, and showed their sharp white teeth, stretching out their claws in a most frightening way.

'Oh, dear!' thought Bobadil. 'Now what am I to do? I daren't call the Prince, or they may jump out at him and kill

him. I wonder where my bunny is. Perhaps he could help me.'

The bunny wasn't very far away. He was still under his bush, watching the cave with wide-open brown eyes. When he saw the cats get up and snarl he guessed that his master was somewhere near, and he called out to warn him.

'Master Wizard!' he cried. 'Be careful, the cats are waiting for you.'

'I know,' said Bobadil. 'I can't think how to get past them.'

'*I'll* help you!' cried the brave little bunny. He suddenly ran out from his bush, and darted just by the two surprised cats. They stood and stared at him, and then, as he came by them again, they both made a dash and tried to spring on him. He was too quick though, and tore off through the wood. Both cats forgot all about guarding the cave entrance, and went tearing after him.

That was Bobadil's chance! He ran out of the cave quickly, and ran to where the Prince was anxiously waiting for him. He hurriedly told him all that had happened, and then looked and listened for the brave rabbit to come back to him. But he didn't come, and Bobadil felt very heavy of heart when he thought that perhaps the bunny had been caught by the two fierce cats.

'We cannot wait here any longer,' he said. 'We must go and rescue the Princess at once. Change clothes with me again, Prince, and go to the tower.'

Quickly the two put on their own clothes once more, and then made their way to the tower. But what a sight met their eyes there!

The tower had been changed, and was three times as high as before, so that the Princess leaning out of the window at the top looked like a speck. She was so far away that they could not hear her voice.

Running round and round the tower was a spiral staircase, and on each step stood a goblin, just like the Red Goblin, but smaller. They carried sharp swords in their hands, and the Prince was astonished when he saw them.

'Alas! Alas!' he said. 'This is the revenge of the Goblin. He has had to go away and leave the Princess, but he has put her in the hands of a hundred or more wicked goblins. Look at them, all standing there. I shall never be able to get past them all!'

'Yes, you will,' said Bobadil. 'Put your invisible cloak tightly round you, Prince, then they won't see you. You can slip up all the stairs without any of them knowing!'

The Prince was full of hope again, and pulled his cloak so tightly round him that not a bit of him was to be seen, and Bobadil only knew where he was by his voice.

'I'm going,' he said. 'I'll be back soon, Bobadil.'

Off he went, and slipped past all the watchful goblins unseen. They heard the patter of his feet, and stared in surprise, but as they could see no one they did nothing.

Up and up went the Prince, up and up, until he came to the top of the tower. Here he found a door, strong and big, closed with a great bar of iron. The Prince was in despair, for he tried to move it and could not. But he remembered his sword, and, taking it up, he hit the door a mighty blow with it. The blade cut through it as easily as a knife cuts cheese, and in one bound the Prince was through it, and saw the frightened Princess.

'It's your Prince!' he cried, catching her up. 'Don't be frightened. I am going to take you away!'

She could not see him, but she knew his voice, and clung to him as he picked her up. At the same moment in came all the goblins, having heard the smashing of the door. They could not see the prince, but when they saw the Princess swung off her feet they knew that a rescuer was there, and ran towards him, waving their swords.

The Prince saw that he could not escape by the stairs, so he jumped onto the windowsill, holding the Princess tightly, and then leapt into the air.

His ankle wings took him safely through the air, and the furious goblins watched the queer sight of the Princess sailing off through the sky, seemingly by herself. Down the stairs they rushed, but they could do nothing.

Bobadil was at the bottom of the stairs looking up at the Princess in great astonishment, having quite forgotten that the Prince was wearing magic wings. There the goblins found him, and at once took him prisoner.

'Hands off me!' said Bobadil. 'I am a wizard, and it was all through me that the Prince was able to rescue his Princess and marry her.'

'*Marry* her!' shouted the goblins. 'But he promised not to.'

'Oh, no, he didn't,' grinned Bobadil. '*I* promised not to marry her, which is a very different thing, isn't it? It was I who was in the Prince's clothes when the twelfth wish was asked.'

Well, the goblins were so astonished when they heard this that they decided to go away and tell their master about it.

'Take him into the very heart of the wood,' said one. 'Leave him there, for he can never find his way out by himself, and we shall easily find him again when we come back.'

So Bobadil was taken to the very

middle of the wood, and left there in the deep shadow of the great trees. He was rather frightened, for he felt quite sure that he never *would* find his way out, and he couldn't quite think what to do.

'If only I were a *real* wizard, instead of just a pretend one,' he groaned. 'I could get out of here as easily as anything. I'm a wizard who isn't a wizard, and now I'm in a regular fix.'

Just at that moment he heard a scurry of little feet, and saw to his great delight his bunny coming scampering towards him.

'The cats got me into a hollow tree!' he panted, 'and it was ever such a long while till they went back to the cave again. Jump on my back, Master Wizard, and I will take you to the Prince's castle.'

Bobadil gladly jumped on the rabbit's soft back, and off they went through the dark wood, till at last they came to a grand castle, guarded by a thousand fine soldiers.

The Prince came running down the steps when he saw the wizard and the

rabbit, and all the soldiers cheered.

'You're just in time for the wedding,' cried the Prince. 'Come along quickly, for I have a hundred bags of gold to give you.'

Bobadil stayed for the wedding, and a very grand affair it was. Then he went on his way again, with a hundred soldiers in front of him, all carrying his bags of gold.

He was very happy when he thought what a fine time he would have when he got home again, and what a grand party he would give to all his friends.

And so he did, but it wasn't very long before he was off on his adventures again, as you will hear another day!